KT-409-164

Who's making that smell?

Philip Hawthorn and Jenny Tyler

Illustrated by Stephen Cartwright

 There is a little yellow duck and a white mouse
to look out for on every double page.

Who's making that smell?
Phheeeeww!!
Behind that screen as well.
It can't be Ben or Annabel.

Who's making that smell?
OOOoooooooohh!!
It could be caramel.
Is it Ben or Annabel?

Who's making that smell?
PoooHH!!
Hey Ben where's Annabel?
Oh, I can hear her yell.

It's certainly not me.

First published in 1994 by Usborne Publishing Ltd, Usborne House, 83-85 Saffron Hill, London EC1N 8RT, England.
Copyright © 1994 Usborne Publishing Ltd.

The name Usborne and the device 🎈 are Trade Marks of Usborne Publishing Ltd. All rights reserved. No part of this publication may be reproduced, stored in a retrieval system, or transmitted in any form or by any means, electronic, mechanical, photocopying, recording or otherwise, without the prior permission of the publisher.

UE
Printed in Singapore
First published in America March 1995

Who's making that smell?

Lots of smells, some nice and some, well, not so nice, but who's making them? Find out by lifting the flaps in this charmingly illustrated book.

The simple rhythmic text is a pleasure to read aloud and young children will enjoy joining in with Ben and Annabel as they proclaim their innocence.

titles in this series:
Who's making that mess?
Who's making that noise?
Who's making that smell?

£ 3.99

C€

ISBN 0 7460 1681 6

Anne Amedro
Tel. 01595 693298
Organisers No.
AME 06162

9 780746 016817 >

JF AMJJASOND/01